A Sudden Puff
of Glittering Smoke

Anne Fine

A Sudden Puff of Glittering Smoke

Illustrated by David Higham

EGMONT

For Vinit

First published in Great Britain 1989
by Piccadilly Press Ltd
Published 1991 by Egmont Books Ltd
239 Kensington High Street, London W8 6SA

Text copyright © Anne Fine 1989
Illustrations copyright © David Higham 1991
Cover illustration copyright © Lee Gibbons 2000

The moral rights of the author, illustrator and cover illustrator
have been asserted.

ISBN 0 7497 0254 0

10 9 8 7 6 5 4 3

A CIP catalogue record for this title
is available from the British Library

Printed and bound in Great Britain
by Cox & Wyman Ltd, Reading, Berkshire

CHAPTER ONE

Jeanie sat at her desk, twisting the ring on her finger round and round. The ring was bothering her terribly. It was so tight she couldn't get it off. She'd only found it a couple of hours before, glinting so brightly in the gutter she was astonished no one else had noticed it. She'd picked it up and looked around, wondering what to do. Then, when the school bell rang, she'd pushed it hastily onto a finger and run the last few yards into the playground.

But in her hurry she had shoved it on the wrong finger. Now she'd been struggling with it all through register.

"Call out your name if you are having a school dinner today," ordered Mr Piper.

"David!"

"Asha!"

"William!"

"Jeanie!"

As she called out her name, she couldn't help giving the ring another little twist.

There was a sudden puff of glittering smoke, and the ring was spinning on the desk in front of her. Jeanie drew her hand away smartly, and stared in wonder.

Before her eyes, the smoke turned to a column of glistening fog, then formed a spinning ball, then took – slowly, slowly – a strange and ancient shape.

It was a genie.

No doubt about it. He was no taller than her pencil and mist still curled around him; but he looked like every genie she had ever seen in books: a little fat in the belly, with a silk bodice and billowing pantaloons that looked for all the world as if they had been woven from silver shifting mists. Tiny stars winked all over them, and they were held up

by a belt of pure gold. On his feet were the tiniest curly slippers, with pointed ends.

Folding his arms, the genie bowed low.

"Greetings," he said.

Jeanie just stared, scarcely believing what she saw. She gave herself a little shake, and looked around the classroom. But nobody else seemed to have noticed this odd little creature standing in a pool of mist on her desk.

Extraordinary!

Was she dreaming? Was it possible? Had some old, old magic come her way?

"Who are you?" she whispered.

"I am the genie of the ring," the small apparition with the folded arms declared. "You called me."

"*I* called you?"

"*Genie*, you called."

"Not G-e-n-i-e! *J-e-a-n-i-e*!"

The creature shrugged.

"One little mistake," he said. "Even a genie gets rusty after five hundred years stuck in a ring."

"Five hundred years!"

Jeanie was horrified. She felt sorry enough for herself, stuck in the classroom all day. But five hundred years stuck in a ring!

The genie, however, simply waved a hand, lightly dismissing whole lifetimes left unlived.

"Where Hope is lost, Patience must reign. In the end there will always be someone."

"And it was me! So now you're *mine*."

The genie looked her up and down coolly, and raised his eyebrows. Jeanie blushed. She wished she had taken the trouble that morning to put on something fancier than her plain shirt and faded jeans. To judge from the shimmering finery the genie wore, he had been used to far better days and far richer places.

But it wasn't her clothes he was noticing, but her bad manners.

"You do not *own* me," he corrected her sternly. "I serve the ring. It just so happens you were wearing it."

Now Jeanie blushed even more deeply.

It was the genie's turn to feel sorry for her.

"Put on the ring," he told her more gently.

"It would be such a shame to lose it now."

Obediently Jeanie picked up the ring from where it still lay in a little cloud of vapour. She slipped it on, and it felt chilly to the touch. She chose a better finger for it this time. It fitted more comfortably than before.

The genie looked up at her, towering over him.

"And now," he said. "Your wish is my wish."

"I wish . . . I wish . . ."

She glanced round the classroom. Everyone else had settled down to work, and Mr Piper was standing by Asha's desk, chatting to her. No one had seen, no one had heard a thing. Clearly the genie was invisible to everyone except the person who had rubbed the ring. Even the conversations with him were somehow silent. No one would ever know what she wished.

She could choose anything in the world. But what? Now that the ring was safe on her finger, she would have plenty of time to think up wonderful wishes to last a lifetime. What should she choose right now, stuck in the classroom?

"I'd like a brilliant day."

"A brilliant day?"

"Yes. I want one of those days when everything I say and everything I do makes people stare at me in amazement."

The genie shook his head, and sighed. But he'd been in the business of granting secret wishes for over seven thousand years. He knew a lot about the human soul. He only said:

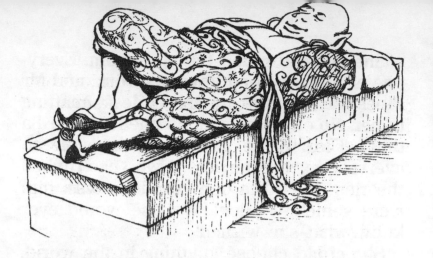

"Your whim is my command."

And then he stretched himself out on the lid of her pencil box, and tucking his hands beneath his head, lay as though sprawled out on golden sands, entirely relaxed, his fat little paunch rising and falling gently with each breath.

Jeanie was a little suspicious. He didn't *look* as if he was organising anything brilliant. But just at that moment Mr Piper began to talk to the class about the fact that it was Asha's last day, she was leaving for India.

"Flying home to the sun," said Mr Piper, waving at the rain beating against the window panes. "Off to a hotter place."

The genie stirred.

"Ah," he murmured. "So many glorious hot places I remember. Arabia. . . Africa. . . India. . ."

"Who can name somewhere else really hot?" asked Mr Piper.

"Where are you from?" Jeanie whispered to the genie.

"Baghdad," he replied, idly crossing one leg over the other and picking at a loose thread in his silver slipper. "It was the shining jewel of all Arabia."

"Baghdad!" called out Jeanie, and added without thinking, "It was the shining jewel of all Arabia."

Mr Piper's eyes widened.

"Well done! And can you tell us anything more about it?"

She glanced down at the genie, still lazing on the desk. Could she?

The genie smiled. Then, gently, he blew. A stream of glittering mist flew up from his mouth and swirled around Jeanie like rings around a planet.

"In the good old days," she heard herself

saying, "Baghdad was truly a city of marvels. Mere words cannot describe its mysteries or its wonders."

Everyone stared. Mr Piper's mouth dropped open. The genie shut his eyes till his dark lashes fluttered on his cheeks, and blew and blew, and Jeanie began to speak of the most magnificent palace from which four highways ran out through massive gateways in high walls, and stretched to the corners of the old Arab empire. She spoke of merchants travelling east and west, and of enormous wealth and terrible poverty. She used words she had never used before – words she had never even heard! She told them about the ruler – Caliph, she called him. She told them about mosques made of finely patterned tiles where Muslims gathered to worship Allah. She spoke of vast bazaars humming with people buying and selling.

"Jeanie!" cried Mr Piper. "You must have spent the whole weekend locked in the library, to know so much!"

Jeanie tried to stop. But the genie still blew. The glittering rings still circled round her head. Without wanting to keep on, she found herself telling Mr Piper all about houses built of sun-dried bricks, whitewashed to hurl the heat of the fierce sun back in its face. She told him about cool hidden courtyards and wooden shutters that kept out the sun by day and the desert winds by night.

"Anyone would think you had lived there all your life!"

She wanted the genie to stop blowing. But his eyes were closed. Oh, he was thousands of miles away – and on Jeanie had to go, telling Mr Piper about young boys with dark and shining eyes who drove their donkeys through the narrow streets, selling their firewood or water from leather bags.

"Shall we stop there for a moment?"

Stop? She couldn't stop. Now she was speaking of the riches of Arabia: perfumes, fleet horses, licorice, coffee –

"Jeanie –"

Too late! Already she was praising all the Arabian scholars who had treasured learning, the mathematicians and architects, the doctors and astronomers and philosophers.

"Jeanie!"

Everyone had turned to look at her. She

must stop. But the magic was too powerful. The genie was still blowing.

"No more!" she implored him silently. "Stop!"

"For the love of Allah!" he cried impatiently, opening his eyes at last. "We've only just begun! You haven't even mentioned the wandering Bedouin tribes who live in tents of camel's hair and move through the blinding desert heat from one cool oasis to another!"

"Stop, please!" Jeanie begged the genie.

"Stop, please!" Mr Piper begged Jeanie.

The genie took no notice. He just blew.

"There is a Bedouin curse," Jeanie told her astonished classmates. "It goes: *May God cause you to live in a city.*"

"That's really interesting, Jeanie," said Mr Piper. "But – "

Jeanie couldn't help interrupting him.

"They are an honourable people, the Bedouin. Even an enemy is given food and shelter for three days. It is a hard life, though it's lived by choice. They – "

"Jeanie!" cried Mr Piper.

14

"Genie!" cried Jeanie.

The genie sat bolt upright, outraged.

"What about all the rest?" he demanded. "*Salaam*, the daily greeting, *Peace*? The treasures and harems and eunuchs and fabulous carpets? The soaring minarets from which the muezzin call the faithful to prayer? The slaves and snake charmers and –"

Reaching down, Jeanie swatted him off the desk.

He fell in a shower of sparks, turning over and over in shimmering somersaults until he reached the floor, silent at last.

There, glowering at Jeanie from between narrowed eyes, he spun round and round on the curled tip of one of his embroidered slippers. Faster he spun – until his features were blurred. *Faster* – until he had become a

glowing ball. *Faster and faster still* – until he was a spinning column of glistening fog.

Then – *puff*! *flash*! He was gone.

For just a moment Jeanie felt the ring on her finger throb and go warm.

Then – nothing.

She breathed again, then looked, a little fearfully, round the class.

Everyone, absolutely everyone, was staring at her in amazement.

* * * *

CHAPTER TWO

She didn't rub the ring to summon the genie back at once. So far he'd made her day a little *too* brilliant. Everyone had been staring at her in the wrong *sort* of amazement. She could do with a break.

The next hour passed with almost no interruption. No puffs of smoke. No angry showers of sparks. Only the ring on her finger getting warm over and over again, as if he were boiling with impatience inside it. So when Mr Piper said at the beginning of Art, "Call out your name if you need a paint jar," it was almost an accident that she was pulling at the hot little circle of gold just as she called out,

"Jeanie."

Puff! Flash! A column of drifting smoke, and he was there again, not bowing quite so deeply as before.

"Your wish?"

Jeanie flushed with annoyance. She felt a fool. It was one thing to conjure up a genie by accident, another to do it quite by mistake.

Unless, of course, you pretend that you did it on purpose. . .

Jeanie waved at her blank sheet of painting paper, and at the suggestion Mr Piper had written on the board: *The Most Beautiful Landscape.*

"Tell me," she said. "Which is the most beautiful landscape you have ever seen?"

The genie needed no prompting.

"Africa," he said. "Africa is *magnificent.* Africa is *dazzling.* Africa is *sublime.*"

"You don't think it might have changed a bit since you last saw it?"

"Changed?" The genie stared. "Can burning plains and rolling grasslands change? Can razor-backed mountains fall flat? Shining waterfalls dry up as they tumble? Can

18

mile on gleaming mile of sun-drenched beach fold up and disappear?"

Well. That seemed clear enough. Jeanie picked up her paintbrush.

"Go on, then," she said. "Fire ahead."

The genie shut his eyes. "Begin," he said, "by painting a lush river valley where comely antelope may dip their slender necks to sip from refreshing waters."

Jeanie was no born painter. Her lush river valley looked like something rather nasty spilled across a garage floor, her antelope like strange, long-eared maggots on peg legs.

Politely, the genie averted his eyes.

"Flamingoes!" he crooned gently, almost to himself, as his rich memories of Africa revived after centuries of sleep. "Tarantulas. Cobras. Pythons. Elephants!"

"I can't do animals," Jeanie complained.

The genie's lip curled.

"A large brown coconut?" he suggested rudely. "Perhaps a yam? Are they beyond my mistress's frail powers?"

Once again, Jeanie felt like swatting him off the desk.

"It's only *animals* I can't paint."

The light of challenge flashed in his eyes.

"Then paint me a tribal chief. Make him a magnificent African prince who wears his ceremonial robes, and armlets of carved wood, leafed with gold. Paint his bride at his side. Sprinkle her with gold dust!"

Jeanie laid down her paintbrush. Sprinkle her with gold dust! For heaven's sake! What did he think they *put* in school paintboxes? She was as cross with him as he was with her.

"*You* do it," she ordered him. "It is my wish. Paint me the dazzling African land-scape, and the prince." Her eyes flashed, just like his. "And, at his side, paint me a lion so real it roars."

"So real it roars?"

"So real it roars!"

"Your whim – "

He didn't even finish. Or, if he did, the words were drowned by the fizz of a starry streak, bright as a comet's tail, which swept through the air and landed on her painting, changing it instantly.

"Grrrrrrrr!"

"Jeanie? Is that you?"

It was a fearsome lion and a fearsome roar, but Mr Piper was looking only at Jeanie.

"Gggrrrrrrrrrrrrr!"

"Jeanie! Please stop that silly noise at once!"

"GGGRRRRRRRRRRRRRR!"

"Jeanie!"

Frantically, Jeanie twisted the ring. "Genie!" she whispered fiercely. "Disappear!"

A shower of sparks, and he was gone. On the desk, only a silly picture of a coconut, and, when she looked up, the whole class staring at her in amazement.

And, once again, it was the wrong sort.

* * * *

CHAPTER THREE

She was pleased and relieved when, half an hour later, Mr Piper strolled up and put the daily scribbled note from the school kitchen down on her desk.

"Jeanie," he said. "Your turn to copy out the lunch menu and help Mrs Handy set the tables."

Good! He couldn't be cross with her still, and it was a job she really enjoyed. She took the clean sheet of paper he offered her, and, reaching for her felt pens, wrote the date brightly across the top. Then, underneath, she copied out in fat and well-shaped letters (much neater than Mrs Handy's):

Shepherds' Pie
Salad
Fruit & Custard

There. Done. But Mrs Handy would not be coming to fetch it for a while. And so, to pass the time, she started decorating her menu around the edges with a delicate curlicue pattern she'd noticed on the genie's silk bodice. And soon her sheet of paper, too, began to look foreign and exotic and – well, yes – Arabian, as though you might raise your eyes from your prayer mat inside some shadowy mosque, and see the very same pattern repeated in cool tiles around the wall.

Thoughtfully she twisted the ring around her finger. It was as if the genie was, in some quite extraordinary way, much closer than she thought. Even in his absence he seemed to be giving her a hand with the border. She was still sitting quietly, twisting the ring round her finger and wondering, when Mrs Handy popped her head around the door.

"Who's helping today?"

"Me! Jeanie!"

Stupid of her not to lift her fingers off the ring as she called out her name! There was a sudden puff of glittering smoke, and the genie floated down onto the menu.

Startled, she snatched her hands back. The sheet of paper tore in half.

"Oh, no!" Jeanie wailed under her breath. "Now look what's happened!"

"A thousand pardons!" The genie was distraught. "Pelt me with desert roses! Starve me! Behead me!"

For heaven's sake! Starve him! Behead him! Jeanie did not even have time to scowl at him properly before Mrs Handy was calling from the doorway:

"Come along. Don't forget to bring the menu."

Obediently, Jeanie hurried towards the door. The genie leaped from desk to desk alongside her in vaporous somersaults, showering sparks over everyone sitting hunched over their workbooks. Nobody even noticed. Just for a moment, Jeanie felt a pang of envy. None of them had to worry about a genie! Why did she?

Ridiculous! Who could regret real magic when it came their way? She'd have a brilliant day. They'd all be staring at her in amazement – the right sort this time! And, as for the silly torn menu, what was a genie for if not to grant her every wish?

"Please," she said to him outside in the corridor. "I wish you'd make me a brand new menu."

"Allah is merciful!" cried the genie. "Lunchtime at last!"

He might have waited five hundred years for a meal, but Jeanie was in a hurry too.

"Quickly! A menu!"

The genie folded his arms, and bowed.

"Your slightest whim. . ."

Puff! *Flash*! The old torn sheet of paper disappeared, and a new menu was in her hand, complete with the very same patterned border. She was about to look at it, just to check, when Mrs Handy turned in the doorway to the lunchroom and reached out to take it.

Mrs Handy stared at Jeanie in amazement – the wrong sort.

"What's *this*?"

"Your menu."

Mrs Handy frowned. "Is it a joke?"

"A joke?" Jeanie was mystified.

Mrs Handy held out the menu, and Jeanie read:

Goat kebabs in a nest of crushed chick peas
Salad of petals of the desert rose
Pomegranates gathered at first blush of dawn

The genie glanced at it too.

"Lash me a thousand times!" he cried. "I have forgotten the olives bathed in essence of frankincense, without which no banquet could claim to be complete!"

Mrs Handy waved the menu in Jeanie's face.

"This isn't supposed to be a *banquet*," she said crossly. "It's a school dinner, and it's shepherds' pie!"

Fortunately for Jeanie, a violent hiss and rattling from the kitchen distracted her, and she rushed off.

The genie looked baffled.

"What does the fading blossom in the flowery apron *mean*?" he demanded. "All shepherds *love* goat kebabs."

"Not here they don't," Jeanie scolded him. "No one in this country eats goat."

"Really?" The genie was astonished. "No one at all?"

"No one at all."

"Strange!" said the genie, and fell into thoughtful silence. He looked, thought Jeanie, just a little bit homesick. But she'd no time to worry about that now.

"Come on. We have to set tables."

She hurried into the lunchroom. The tables were still pushed against the wall, the dishes still in piles on the china trolley, and it was five to twelve!

Well, what was the point of having a genie if he didn't help?

"Quick," she said. "Push all those tables together and lay out china."

The genie's eyes widened.

"Do my foolish ears deceive me?"

"Don't argue," Jeanie said. "Just lay out china."

The genie bowed.

"Your whim is my command."

The flash that filled the room was so brilliant it blinded Jeanie for a moment. She heard the windows rattle and felt the floor rock. Even to someone as unused to magic as she was, it seemed an awful lot of fuss to get a few plates laid on a few tables.

Warily she opened her eyes – and stared in horror.

The genie had pushed the tables together, and laid out China!

There was no doubt about it. It was China.

From the paper lanterns to the pagodas, from the bamboo to the beansprouts, from the moustaches to the mandarins, it was China. Here, at one end, coolies were working in the flooded paddy fields. There, at the other, there was a tiny city. The curving rooftiles of the houses shadowed the miniature courtyards with their willow trees and clematis and camellias, their lotus pools and fish-ponds full of golden carp. And inside the tiny little houses, sitting amongst the silk hangings and the painted screens, were elegant women with long pins through their hair, and children in brightly-coloured quilted jackets.

From somewhere in the busy little city, a gong rang out loudly.

Mrs Handy's voice came through the dinner hatch.

"Stop ringing that dinner bell. I'm not quite ready yet."

Panicking, Jeanie swung round on the genie.

"Get rid of it!"

The genie seemed as hurt as he was astonished.

"Get rid of it? You haven't even *looked* at it properly yet. You haven't peeped through the windows to look at the the pottery figurines, or the porcelain vases, or the jade carvings. You haven't tasted any of the food."

Somersaulting onto a rooftop, showering sparks, he waved a hand.

"These people are eating too, you know. Bear's paw and baked owl and panther's breast. Not to mention all the boring old plain dishes like lotus roots and bamboo shoots and water chestnuts."

"Clear it away!"

Was he being deliberately awkward? He

took no notice of her pleas as he leaped effortlessly in a sprinkle of stars from one sloping rooftop to another.

"Got any aches and pains?" he taunted her. "The finest acupuncturist in Peking lives here. He'll take his long slim silver needles and – "

"Get rid of it!"

"You haven't even peeked in the opium den yet. . ."

Jeanie was furious.

"Make China disappear! I wear the ring! It is *my wish!*"

A scowl. Another blinding flash. The windows rattled in their frames. The floor rocked. China disappeared.

The hatch flew open.

"What *is* going on?"

"Sorry!" called Jeanie. She looked round for the china trolley. There was nothing on it.

She turned on the genie in a rage.

"Bring back that china!"

China immediately reappeared, with sampans floating down the Yangtze river.

"No, not that China! The *other* china!"

Jeanie was desperate. From the kitchen she could hear the sound of saucepans being scraped.

The genie smiled – not very pleasantly. And only as the hatch swung open and the clock hand reached twelve did he deign to wave a haughty hand.

Instantly, china plates lay in rows of military precision down both sides of the five tables.

"Ring the bell," called out Mrs Handy.

This was the job that everyone loved best. Jeanie ran for the bell. But even before she managed to lay a finger on it, the deep reverberations of an ancient Chinese gong rang through the room.

Jeanie spun round on him.

"You're spoiling everything!" she hissed.

"You and your magic! I think you're a whole lot more trouble than you're worth!"

The genie simply smiled, folded his arms, and bowed.

* * * *

CHAPTER FOUR

What could you do with a genie who hadn't had a meal for five hundred years? You couldn't order him back in a ring, could you? She had to take a chance and let him stay.

And it wasn't as bad as she expected. The first few moments were the worst. As Mrs Handy put the serving dish down on the table top, he came as close as he dared to its hot side, and stood on tip-toe peeping over the rim at the huge mound of shepherds' pie.

Tears sprang to his eyes like two bright little jewels, and he clutched his belly in all the torment of the oriental gourmet who has missed banquet after banquet for centuries, and then been offered lumpy mashed potato.

But he behaved. She didn't have to put up with him leaping in showers of silvery sparks around her plate. And the food was invisible from the moment he scooped it up in his fingers. She didn't see any of the other people at her table staring in astonishment as lumps of shepherds' pie rose in the air and vanished.

"My last school dinner!" said Asha, pushing her plate away. "Tomorrow I shall be in India."

The genie dropped the lump of potato he was holding, and sank to his knees beside Jeanie's plate.

"In–di–a!" It was a sigh of longing. "Oh, Allah! Be merciful! Transport me on the wings of my desire! Oh, India! How many times have I visited you – sweet land of pungent spices. Saffron! Coriander! Tamarind! Turmeric! Cardamom!"

Now the tiny little fellow was trying to push Jeanie's plate further away from him with his foot.

"Believe me, for one brass bowl of fragrant biriani, for one delicious chapati, I'd trade a bullock's cart of this pale mush my mistress offers me!"

"The food's so *different* in India," Asha said. "I've enjoyed my time here, but I shall be glad to be home again."

"Home!" mourned the genie. "Oh, Allah! Arabia, Africa, India – fly me anywhere you choose! The lush green valleys or the burning plains. The crowded cities or the cold high mountains. Anywhere but here!"

He sounded so sincere and desperate that Jeanie could scarcely bear it.

"I don't think any place is really better than another," she said aloud, hoping to console him.

"Home's home," said Asha.

"And blessings are surely heaped upon all those places without grey skies and mashed potato," added the genie.

Jeanie turned her face away. Outside, the rain beat steadily against the window panes. It must, she thought, be terrible to grow up, like Asha and the genie, in sun and heat and

baking dust, only to find yourself stuck in some chill damp place you'd never known.

As terrible as being raised with cool rain on your face and green underfoot, to find yourself in some scorched land where water was more precious than gold, and fierce sunlight hurt your eyes.

She'd hate that. She'd absolutely *hate* it. She'd be so homesick she would *die*.

Jeanie tore off the ring.

"Here!" she said to Asha. "Take it."

"*Take* it?"

"Yes. It's a present. It's for you. Take it. Put it on."

Everyone was staring at her in amazement.

"Please," she begged. "I want you to have it. I want to be able to think of you wearing it in India."

Asha spread her hands shyly.

"I couldn't. It's too – "

The genie was on his knees, pleading silently.

Jeanie gave the ring one last, tiny, secret rub.

"I *wish* you'd take it."

No one else saw the sudden puff of glittering smoke, or heard the genie's sigh of ecstasy. But they all saw Asha reach out as though bewitched, and, taking the ring, slip it on her slim brown finger.

The genie turned to Jeanie. Folding his

arms, he gave his deepest bow in deepest gratitude. The look on his face was wonderful to see. Jeanie could tell that he was already lost in imagination, knowing his years of lonely imprisonment were over forever, and he would find himself spinning to glittering life time and again in cool courtyards and under shady banyan trees.

"Who gave you that?" people would forever be asking Asha.

"This ring?" She'd rub it without thinking. "Oh, *Jeanie*."

And there he'd be, folding his arms and bowing, ready to serve. Until the day the ring slipped off her finger, and he moved on. What had he said? *There will always be someone. . .*

She could have kept him longer. But it would be like keeping a skylark in a tiny cage. Genies were creatures of colour and adventure. She'd read the Arabian Nights. You couldn't expect a genie who had known Sinbad the Sailor and Ali Baba and the forty thieves and Aladdin to be content with rainy skies and mashed potato.

No. Let him go, and wish him well on his travels back to India. . . Africa. . . Arabia. . . So many glorious hot places.

* * * *

CHAPTER FIVE

"In honour of Asha's last day," declared Mr Piper, "we shall all write about India."

Was it the pictures he lifted up to show them wind-whipped desert sands, and the moon hanging like a curved blade over ancient walls?

Or was it the genie secretly blowing one of his magical glittering circles around her head?

For it seemed like a memory, what Jeanie found herself writing about – afternoons so hot and still it seemed that you might run a sword through the air and part it like a thick curtain. It seemed like a memory, what she wrote about the monsoon – the hot winds blowing day and night from the huge open plains, then clouds that banked up till you could hardly bear the sense of waiting any longer. And then suddenly the rains came down with all the force of stones, until the ground sprang lush and green all around, and life burst out, with frogs and toads hopping in hundreds. Snakes! Cockroaches! And a million insects!

She'd never written so much in her life.

After she'd finished, Mr Piper picked it up, and read it aloud to everyone.

"Marvellous!" he kept saying. "Wonderful!"

Asha was staring into space, as if she were already home. The bell rang for the end of school, but everyone sat enchanted in their seats, as Mr Piper read on about the chime of temple bells and the sweet smell of incense and strings of flowers. And women in silk saris with silver bangles tinkling on their wrists and ankles, and ancient dances so precise there are a hundred separate movements for hands and eyes. And carpet weavers, snake charmers, basket makers. And holy men and horoscopes. And sweets and festivals. Everything – everything you might miss if you were far away for five hundred years.

And, as they listened, everyone stared at Jeanie in amazement – the right sort this time.

"Brilliant!" breathed Asha. "That is *exactly* how it is!"

Mr Piper patted Jeanie on the back.

"Well done. Well done!"

As Asha packed up her few things, the ring on her finger seemed to be glowing. Jeanie couldn't help glancing at it a little wistfully. But why be sorry she was letting him go? He'd made things awkward for her all day long. He'd never fit in – not in his growing fever of homesickness. He'd be a lot more trouble than magic was worth.

And he had granted her wish. He'd given her a brilliant day. He'd done his very best. Goodbye and good luck to him.

Just then, Asha came up to say goodbye.

Jeanie smiled as she squeezed the hand that wore the precious ring.

"Good luck. Goodbye." she said. "Goodbye. Good luck."

You'd think, to hear her, she was parting from two people, not just one.

And the ring glowed on Asha's finger as she walked out.

* * * *